I Wont Give Up!

Infinite Reasons to Live!

BY

Naveen Mehta

ISBN 978-93-5438-927-6

Published in India 2021 by Pencil

A brand of
One Point Six Technologies Pvt. Ltd.
123, Building J2, Shram Seva Premises,
Wadala Truck Terminal, Wadala (E)
Mumbai 400037, Maharashtra, INDIA
E connect@thepencilapp.com
W www.thepencilapp.com

AUTHOR BIOGRAPHY

This is my Real Life story and a story of becoming Man from a Boy next door. Its more of my personal Diary which i wrote when i was fighting Cancer. How life keep on throwing challenges at you and only option life give to you is fight. It not an mercy document but i just want to share my thoughts so as some where some one fighting cancer may get some clues to fight his cancers.

CONTENTS

INTRODUCTION

I am 35 year old Indian male. Married and Parent of 5 year old son. I am qualified engineer and was neither a chain smoker nor drinker; you can say I was a moderate smoker and occasional drinker. I was working for an MNC in Mumbai. My first company after my qualification, small but with nice group of people like everybody else I was a dreamer wanted to do best job and engineer, so something different was always going on in my mind. I am only son of my parents and from middle class Indian society. Middle class dreams big and is backbone of Indian economy. My father served in Indian Defence Services and with armed force background, fighting Spirit was something which I inherited from my father. I was a mediocre in studies but always appreciated for extracurricular activities. I used to read a lot and gathering information on new technology is something I always like. Life was going on well...and I was concentrating on my work. Totally unaware of the storm heading towards me I was working and enjoying my life.

THE FIRST SIGNAL

It was a nice day; I had shifted to new city my office headquarters and was staying there without my family. With group of few office friends there was a plan for evening party. All started well and we were enjoying. All was going well and after dinner I went to wash room and noticed something. A big lump of tissue under my tongue and it was bleeding. Ohm...I have never expected this. I brush my teeth everyday and never noticed this earlier, I was surprised. What is this, I was worried and called my family and discussed they suggested I must see my doctor.

MY FIRST MISTAKE

I was afraid and knew that it's something big, and my mind was not accepting this. I neglected it for few months (my first mistake) regretted it later. Things moves on and I kept ignoring it my heart was not accepting the fact. Even before seeing my doctor I was sure this is not good. At last I made up my mind and met one doctor. Doctor said, do you have insurance, I said yes, he replied I will remove this in a day. Doctor got it but didn't tell me anything. I didn't go back to the doctor again. I took leave of few days and visited my hometown around 2000 km from my working city. I met my family and we went to one of my uncle who is a radiologist and he saw the lump and told me you must see one specialist as soon as possible. And I returned to my working city with my wife, and decided to see specialist at the earliest.

THE CONFIRMATION

We went to one of the ENT surgeon in Mumbai, and I have shown him my tongue . He got it but didn't told me anything and told me that they will remove the lump and send it for testing and also they wanted to perform minor surgery as my nasal passage was also unlocked. We took appointment for the operation and left. After few days in month of March 2012, doctors conducted their first operation. They took the lump out and performed nasal surgery. They told us to send the tissues for testing. After 3 days at the hospital I was not able to eat, relaxed but bit worried as I was expecting something... After discharge I collected my biopsy report and went to meet the doctor. Doctor saw the report and final confirmed I have carcinoma of tongue i.e. tongue cancer...we were shocked and didn't know what to do...doctors said he has to discuss further with doctors panel and will let us know about the future course of action. We took a taxi back to home and didn't spoke to each other and reached home. We were shocked it was time for dinner and we didn't want to eat. We were worried and were not sure how to tell our parents about this. I switched on the television and the day was cricket world cup finals and India was fighting to win. Even though I was absent minded something in my heart said...now you have to fight to win for your life and lot of things at stake.... India won that day, everyone was celebrating and I can able to hear the sound of crackers...I did slept that night and was ready to face the challenge ahead or you can say there was no other option..

THE SECOND SURGERY

Once it was confirmed that I have carcinoma, I had to go for further treatment and now the search started for right surgeon. We went to one of top government aided hospital and what I saw was something I can't explain in few words..thousands of people all age groups all suffering from cancer were lying here and there...few doctors and lack of facility to handle crowd in thousand was the problem. Any hospital can't plan for thousands of patients daily...that day I realised I am not alone, millions are fighting this war. We decided to move to other surgeon and next few days gone in discussing about right treatment and doctor. At last we finalised and it was decided that, next surgery doctors will remove around 25 to 50% of tongue and will decide only while operating. There was a possibility; I was not able to speak properly for rest of my life. Doctor told me everything before operating. And then the d day comes...early morning they operated and removed 25% of my tongue. Also they operated my neck and as a precautionary measure and removes few nodes from my neck. After operating I was shifted to my room and I was not able to talk. I had to stay there for next one week. My parents joined me there, they kept my confidence high. In between I had few visitors daily. I was confident and started reading a lot in hospital just to divert my mind.

THE CHALLENGE

My next challenge was to stay without speaking and eating for next one month. I had to stay on liquid for as long as wound heals and have to start talking slowly. Everyday my wife used to bring a glass of liquid food, soup or even grinded and liquefied food to eat. Initially it was fine and later I wanted to eat and speak. In those days I realised, how difficult it is to stay without talking...it was difficult and a challenge which I won't forget in my lifetime. Every day I had to fight my emotions. I had to...for my wife I knew she is worried and didn't want to increase her sufferings because of me. I realised in those days..That when such thing happens I was not worried about myself but I was concerned about my family's future. It's a challenge because million of negative thoughts come in your mind and you know..In order to stay positive you have to fight every negativity in your life.

LIFE COME BACK ON TRACK

After a month of fighting my life started coming on the track..I had started eating solid food and good thing was...I was talking and was sure to talk properly in next few days. It happened and I started talking and rejoin my job. There was support from seniors at office..They have kept it a secret and even I didn't tell it to anybody. I didn't even tell it to many of my relatives and friends.

There was weekly meeting with doctor and I was told there is no permanent cure of cancer and even one single cell again can grow into a tumour again. I had to go for regular checkups. I was praying it should not return again.. But it can...there was every possibility. This was also a challenge as you know it can happen again and started thinking about lot of possibilities. At one point you also accept and move on..even knowing life won't remain same now onwards.

FIGHT FOR INSURANCE

Now as life was coming on track, other reality comes into picture. As I was medically insured by my company, I have submitted my documents for claim. That day I realised how difficult it is to get your money back from these companies. You can pay your insurance premiums online and even there agents come to your house to collect the cheque but when it comes to claiming your insurance...in India it's a hell for medical insurers. Insurance company usually hires a third party to settle claims and these agents are big b**** they keep on asking for new document s and even some time wants to confirm your illness. It was a hell...they paid up 60% of my first claim after a year. And didn't play for my second treatment and wanted me to prove my disease. I was not in a position to visit there heading office daily...so I stepped back. That day I realised Insurance is one thing but you should have sufficient cash balance to meet adversities. In India you can't just rely on these companies..They are just minting money. You should save some amount every month to handle this adversity. I would definitely name the company it was the agent of national assurance company of India, the ttk healthcare services. This company has office across India but when it comes to claiming they are big bas****. This cheap language is for all of these companies which take advantage of government guidelines and playing with thousands of people. They have a dedicated call centre but these people and their software are of no use. Sometimes I guess may be these third party get some rewards from main insurance companies to save their money. And also..Maybe they wanted customers to visit there office personally so the government corrupt staff can get commission from common man indirectly. I visited one of their offices..They said sir is now out of office..You want your money you can contact him on his personal number. It was fishy and obviously like millions I had to return back empty-handed.

MISTAKE 2

Another mistake which I made was I had not sufficiently insured myself. Medically I was only insured by my employer and I had no individual mediclaim policy. This mistake most of us make when we are young. We think we are fine, healthy and no regular diseases when we are young and we don't insure our self. Another mistake most of us make is we don't insure our self sufficiently. I had insurance but that was not sufficient to take care of increasing healthcare expenses, so insufficiently insured is as bad as uninsured. And I came to know that, now that I have a critical illness I can't insure myself for the disease for next four years. A lesson was you should insure your family for more than 5 times of current expenses of critical illness. Suppose current expenses for cancer is 5 lac in India then you should insure your family for around 25 lacs. Researching online and through your contacts research and insure your family. And also cross check claiming procedure and process.

2012 TO 2014

I was on regular monthly checkups and everything was fine. There were no sign of tumour and as days passed by I was forgetting it and was concentrating on my work. But it was a challenging period I got caught in some cheap office politics..And my boss who was only aware of my disease started taking advantage of it and building pressure on me to quit, he has used all his resources and tactics to show me the exit door. I knew I had to quit one day but he my boss was an another cancer I was fighting. People usually say western people are racists but reality is India is an racist society, so many religion, casts, colours, languages etc. and people are generally racist. I say I was not because I came from a background where it is taught to celebrate and respect all religions, casts, colours etc. My father's defence services environment taught us that. My boss was racist...he used to trust only his religion guys and was engineer with dumb brain and not at all creative. He was earning good and wanted others to stop thinking and keep on working. It can be true with other professions but not with engineers, even if you are top school graduate, if you can't think differently you are not an engineer at all. This was happening I got zero increments as they knew I am down, won't quit them. I was the same guy rewarded with best performance for three years and now I was not a performer. It did hurt but I was waiting for right time to quit. And one odd day my inner voice told me to quit and I had to quit for sake of my respect. Now it was a great challenge, medical expenses and no job. I had to do something and I decided to start my own work and simultaneously started searching for another job. It didn't end there..Few people want to interfere in your life even after you leave them. And now my ex boss was becoming revengeful I don't know why? May be because I disrespected him before quitting or may be because of some other pressures...

They started interfering in my personal life. They become fake callers for job or business and started taking advantage of me.

They were on head hunting and wanted me to teach lessons. I knew that and ultimately they were successful in their efforts and hired me for one third company where they can teach me a lesson. The company was an Indian entity with international clients, they are big time agents for few MNC in India (I won't name these companies as investigations are still on and I have ethics unlike them and I won't divert from my ethics) they officially pick people and use tricks to teach them lessons obviously for their clients following all government guidelines. That day I realised how and why we Indians were slaves for years...it was our mistake...we are weak..Our society and people were not strong ethically and started fighting themselves and few business men from Europe took advantage and turned us into slaves...I must say many of us are still slaves by choice. I was hired but given no task...I had to sit ideal for 8 hrs in closed room and every month I have been told you are not performing. It didn't affect me at all..But I was worried for many other people with whom these companies play. Also one thing I learned was for sake of money 99% of people can do anything...just to save their jobs and position some good managers are wasting there talents with these type of companies. Only for money human bring can go to any extent. I realised and was sure there is something fishy and disclosed companies and people information to few people in government using my resources. Now as I was sure of action on these people and companies I had to quit my job again...it was a fight and for no reason you have to fight them there was no other choice. And I have been suggested to leave the city Mumbai and I left for my home town...obviously without a job. But I was courageous enough to handle these things and was ready for new beginning in new place. And I realised there are indirect cancers around you they will try to intervene in your system and like a warrior only option is to remove them from system. I realised now I have to fight many cancers in my lifetime and as always I was ready.... and this time prepared.. As they say when you strike your enemy..You strike them hard...and I was committed to strike my cancers hard. India is always known for peace and prosperity...we don't strike our enemies first. But when we strike, we strike really hard and world had seen it. Now as a common man I had to prove I am Indian by heart and now as the enemy intervened I have to strike hard. I reached my home town..It is a small town and there are not much opportunities and it took me a while to get another job near my hometown. It was a manufacturing plant with lot of work. I was concentrating on my job and getting used to day to day lifestyle. Problem here was I can't visit my doctor monthly and as it is a small town so no oncologist in the town. I had to travel to near my capital city for follow-ups. But nobody can guess about future and I knew this...somewhere back in mind daily I am worried of it.

IT RETURNS

One fine day I was checked my mouth and found some harshness, it was not like previous one but area of my tongue was hard.

I was afraid and worried...didn't tell it to anybody and decided to see doctor again. I was also not able to speak properly and my voice was not clear. Everybody got it...there is something not right. We went to one of the doctor and he was also sure that it returned but wanted to crosscheck it and suggested us to go for the test. We went for MRI scan and got the report very next day and now it was confirmed that it returned. At new place in tongue and doctors called it a new primary. This time my wife was shocked and depressed because in last three years we had somewhat adjusted and life was on track. Again meeting with doctors started and few suggested going for surgery and few suggested going for chemotherapy and radiation. It was a big confusion and we had to decide. I had no insurance now and treatment was very expensive this time. We met many doctors and ultimately it was decided that we will go for chemotherapy and radiation cycles. The Fight Begun Again

The fight has started and my enemy surfaced again and no option left...only option is to fight it out again.

Treatment was Radiation therapy daily and weekly chemotherapy cycles.

Radiation Therapy starts with construction of face mask for radiation on effected area, as the affected area was neck so they made a mask by putting some kind of hot material on my face then it solidified and took shape of my face.

Radiation therapy is painless, everyday you have to visit radiation department, they put you on a machine for few minutes under high intensity x-rays.

But it does effects the cells and I started getting ulcers in my mouth. As days passed ulcers increased and now I was back on liquids...liquids that to only sweet..No salty liquids.

Worst thing started after 15days, I was not able to drink even plain water I had to add sweetener to it. It was worst I started losing weight.

Chemotherapy was also going on simultaneously, in this they were injecting medicines in my body one a week for 8 hrs.

Strange thing was your body stay healthy..Whoever comes to see you doesn't able to make out what's the problem is...only I know what I was feeling.

Everybody from my family, especially my wife stood by me and kept on motivating me...she was also going through indirect pain which I can't explain. I had to again take break from my job..So almost jobless..My wife also was not able to work as she has to be with me for whole day.

Radiation and Chemotherapy was a 35 days treatment and after the treatment end my mouth wad swollen from inside...I had to go through many pains.

I was not eating for a month and so was very week and was not able to walk properly. Doctors said they can only tell us about results after few months because everything was swollen in my mouth and the available technology can't make out anything at that time.

We returned to our home town...I was only on liquids and few medicines. Now it was another challenge I had to eat painkillers to sleep properly in night and whole day stay at home and somehow keep my confidence high. At this time as you are ideal...many things started hitting your mind and only thing it required was patience. Family was also going through their worst phase, her son was on bed and for my wife her husband was ill and she has to bear my mood swings. It still hurts me how one man's diseases effects whole people around him.

Anyhow my wife resumed work and my father was getting his pension post retirement. so thing were still moving. Three months passed and I was still on liquids. Things were improving but Very slowly after three months I started having some semisolid food that to only sweet...I can't tell you how difficult it is to live without eating for so long.

Any how things improved and I went through another test and this time..I have been told that still I have to wait for few more months and then they will test me again.

I lost my job again, as I was not able to join office for more than 6 months...my hr staff came to my home and asked for resignation..As it was there rule...obviously I had to accept it and I resigned..They assured me that I can apply back once I am fit. I knew those who came to my house were showing me exit door..and are only employees..They have to do what their boss wanted them to do. It's a private company..It's there policy and I can't do anything about it. Realised, why we don't have government defined policies for hr even for private companies.

This time I was not dejected...I was happy to leave this company. I had many other things to concentrate on.

2015

It's a new year and my health was coming back on track and I am still waiting for my next test...now I am able to eat slowly and some food without spices and masalas...but its improving day by day. And also I have started writing..Which I never did in my lifetime...but had to do now..This is what god wants..I am writing..And not too good in English. But I hope my words are reaching you...you are able to guess what happen to me and many other people fighting this disease around world. Don't be afraid...it is only to let people understand and be prepared to face worst situations. It can hit anyone of us and you should learn from others mistake.

HOW TO FIGHT CANCER

In this book I will Jot down few strategy which I have applied in my fight against cancer. Goal is to help somebody learn from my experience and strategies. I am writing this for 1 person, yes! Even if 1 person in this world can learn something to fight his cancer from this book my mission is accomplished.

1. Cry it out!

First thing which you must do when doctor disclose you that you have cancer is just keep you calm at hospital and come back home calmly...yes, try to keep your emotions in control and come back to home and disclose the news to your loved one but stay calm don't panic in front of them as keeping your loved one emotions in control is your responsibility. Then go to your room or and CRY it out yes, cry as much as you can but alone as crying will relieve you from tense mental pressure yes take all your negativity through tears. I think when I diagnosed with cancer I didn't cried but later I felt that I must have cried a bit because it's important to follow god rules when you have some negative punches in your life basically god want you to cry and take your negative emotions out.

So what I have learned that you must cry and take out the negative punch which you have got from god...if he is punching you and want you to cry then we must cry a bit.

2. Stop Crying and Start Thinking

Yes one day is enough for crying to take negativity out. Now you must stop crying and start thinking. First you must stop blaming yourself or god for this entire thing. You must take is as it's in your destiny and it has to happen. Now think why god has given you this and what he want you to do. Did he want you to cry No! Did he want to punish No! Did he want you to kill yourself absolutely No! He wants you to fight...Yes! He wants you to fight and set an example to others in your life to get inspired and clap on your effort. Yes god wants you to fight...he has given you a challenge and now it's you who has to decide whether you want to fight or give up! In My case I choose to fight. I chose to fight in a way that someday my children's and loved ones will say...yes what a man I am and what a fight I fought. Yes in my case I decided to fight to set an example for my kid...may be I will live or die it's in god hands but I will fight it in the way that nobody else ever fought. Yes this approach I opted to fight for the greatest battle of my life.

3. Accept the reality

Yes you must accept the reality that all of us will die ...we all will die someday few will die of disease and few will die by accident but in end death is the biggest reality and we must accept this fact. Now as we have decided to not cry and think and ready to fight...we must accept that cancer is never ending fight you have to keep on fighting all your life some time to cure it and someday to fight post cure side effects. It's a never ending fight which now you have to fight every second. Accept that even a single cell can again re grow to become cancer again so you have to stay vigilant it will test you mentally, physically and whatever way you can imagine

In all you must accept the reality.

4. Start Fighting

Yes now after 2 days, you are bit confident and now back on your feet again after crying. Now start fighting, start with some basic researching on net about your cancer, and don't research too much. Just research enough which will keep you motivated. Basically you are trying to just learn what you are suffering from so that you understand your disease and be bit prepared when you meet your doctor. Now here opinion of your close loved ones...tell them frankly to not de motivate you and help you stay positive in your fight...this is helpful because you will find many who will cry in front of you but telling them frankly basically you are drawing a wall which protect you from de motivation. Now start meeting doctors and just here there opinion. yes just here there opinion and meet many doctors but please only the best in your budget. Ask them what is the cure? What is the treatment? What's the cost? Etc. Basically you are collecting information and after collection of information sit with someone close at home and try to analyze gathered information and decide on doctor, a treatment which doctors suggested. Cost of treatment again is a big concern so better on the side keep on checking you budget and insurance etc. in case you are not insured try to think where you can raise money from. Even of you are from poor family don't ever de motivate yourself because truth is every government has best doctors and cost of treatment is subsidized in government hospitals but yes you have to run a bit. Don't think you ont get best treatment there. If you can't afford private treatment just go to for government hospital don't worry just research a bit more on all government hospitals meet as many doctors in government hospitals as you can. One more thing which you can take an idea is, if you can't afford private treatment even then you must visit all doctors and get there opinion and yes tell them truth afterwards that you can afford treatment in there hospital and believe me 90% of them will give you better suggestions for treatment in government hospital. Here they collect information they give you and analyze and take a final decision where you will get treatment. Doesn't waste too much time in this entire do it as fast as possible because time is very crucial in fight against cancer.

One thing you might noticed above while writing above paragraphs weather I got time to worry...No I was motivated and too busy in fight and basically didn't have much time to think. This is for me the best way to stop worrying and start doing.

5. During Treatment

After you have decided the treatment and hospital, now time is to move in next phase of treatment. Again don't think to much and start doing what your doctors say yes blindly follow the doctor, now he is your savior. Take name of your lord, pray to him that oh my god! Give me courage and blessing in my fight and tell him that now he is your savior and this doctor is just an meant your god want to help you with. Trust god, trust doctor and just be motivated and jump into treatment. During treatment you will have many small pains and you will be afraid of looking at other people sufferings or may be from machines etc. but now you have to stay motivated by listening to songs , talking to loved one or just watching TV in hospital or may be going to cafeteria and have some healthy food. Basically the trick is to divert your attention from all de motivating things around you. Whenever you come back from hospital during treatment just relax and do everything to divert your attention from all negativity in your life. Watch TV; Read books, Watch War movies any motivational thing you can do.

Core is to keep yourself motivated analyze yourself, whatever motivates you and do that

6. Post Treatment

After treatment in most cases cancer is treated but reality is cancer is never ending fight you have to fight every second for rest of your life and its better you accept. Post treatment there is always a chance of cancer recurring so better be prepared always. Jot down your strategy again, do what doctors say and follow their instructions. Don't think too much because only thing in your hand is to fight and you must keep on fighting. Most people lost their jobs or earnings post cancer , they must again try to stand up on their feet , the best way is to open up tell your career problems to your relatives, friends and everybody you think can help you again stand up again. May be you might be earning much earlier don't be ashamed to get low paying job, because your first priority must be to stand up again and start earning again. In all this you must enjoy and thank god for the second chance he has given you. You must carry on with your daily activities of motivating yourself and keep on your fight.

7. Conclusion

Cancer is something you must not be afraid of 90 percent cases if detected earlier can be treated. Don't be afraid if you are diagnosed with cancer; fight it out because that is the only option god has given you. Stay Motivated and Enjoy you fight.

www.ingramcontent.com/pod-product-compliance
Lightning Source LLC
LaVergne TN
LVHW050429160726
843469LV00041B/1291

9789354389276